Mom's Little Instruction Book

The Wise and Witty World of Motherhood

Annie Pigeon

P
PINNACLE BOOKS

PINNACLE BOOKS are published by

Windsor Publishing Corp.
475 Park Avenue South
New York, NY 10016

The P logo Reg. U.S. Pat. & TM Off. Pinnacle is a trademark of Windsor Publishing Corp.

First Printing: April, 1994

Printed in the United States of America

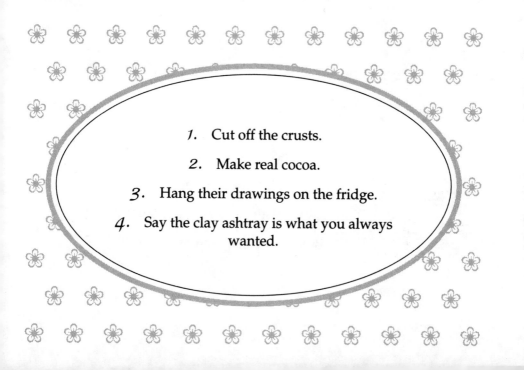

1. Cut off the crusts.

2. Make real cocoa.

3. Hang their drawings on the fridge.

4. Say the clay ashtray is what you always wanted.

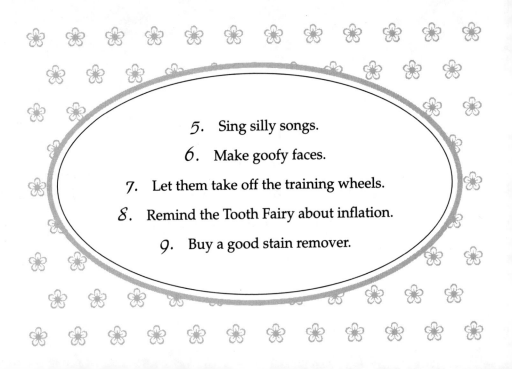

5. Sing silly songs.

6. Make goofy faces.

7. Let them take off the training wheels.

8. Remind the Tooth Fairy about inflation.

9. Buy a good stain remover.

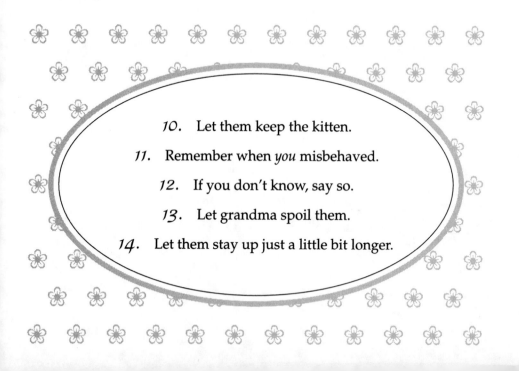

10. Let them keep the kitten.

11. Remember when *you* misbehaved.

12. If you don't know, say so.

13. Let grandma spoil them.

14. Let them stay up just a little bit longer.

15. Lock up the good china.

16. Tickle.

17. Be a good sport.

18. Be a good friend.

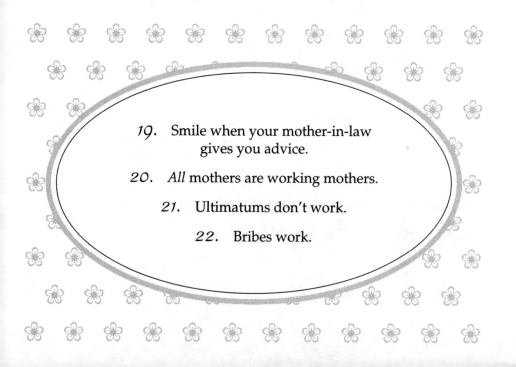

19. Smile when your mother-in-law gives you advice.

20. *All* mothers are working mothers.

21. Ultimatums don't work.

22. Bribes work.

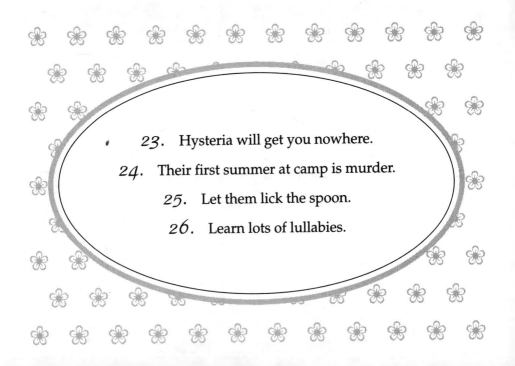

23. Hysteria will get you nowhere.

24. Their first summer at camp is murder.

25. Let them lick the spoon.

26. Learn lots of lullabies.

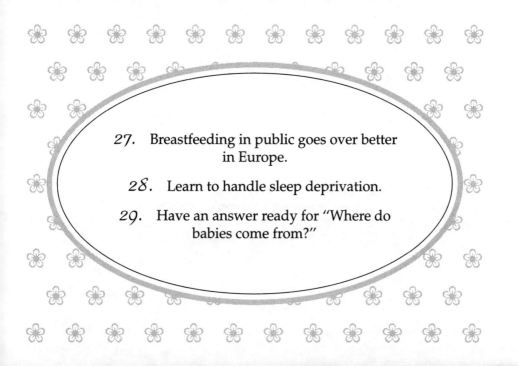

27. Breastfeeding in public goes over better in Europe.

28. Learn to handle sleep deprivation.

29. Have an answer ready for "Where do babies come from?"

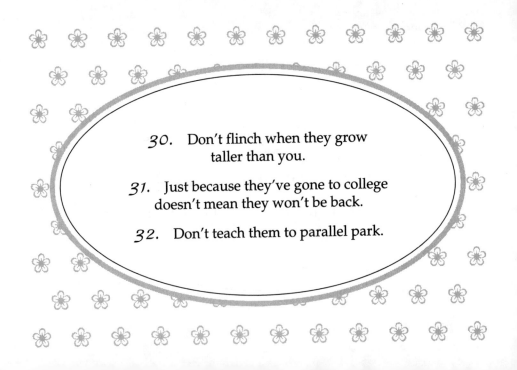

30. Don't flinch when they grow taller than you.

31. Just because they've gone to college doesn't mean they won't be back.

32. Don't teach them to parallel park.

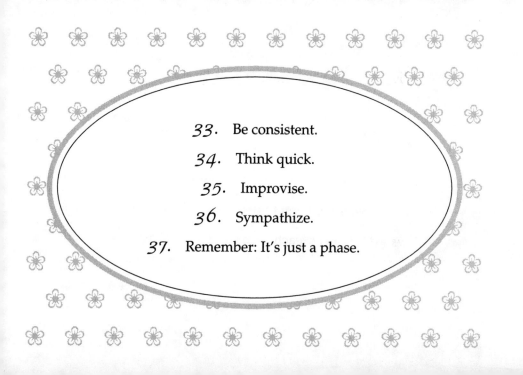

33. Be consistent.

34. Think quick.

35. Improvise.

36. Sympathize.

37. Remember: It's just a phase.

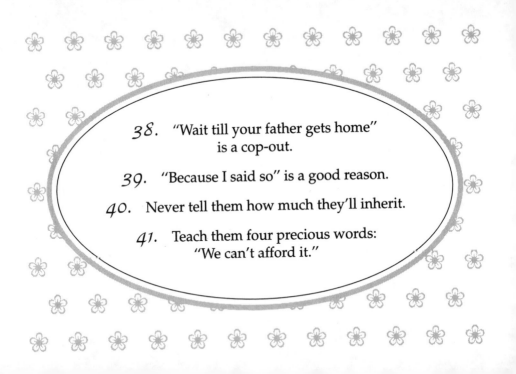

38. "Wait till your father gets home" is a cop-out.

39. "Because I said so" is a good reason.

40. Never tell them how much they'll inherit.

41. Teach them four precious words: "We can't afford it."

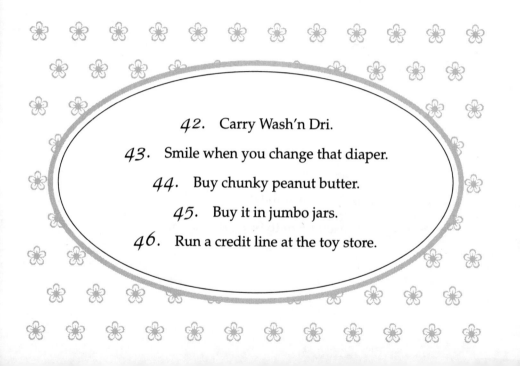

42. Carry Wash'n Dri.

43. Smile when you change that diaper.

44. Buy chunky peanut butter.

45. Buy it in jumbo jars.

46. Run a credit line at the toy store.

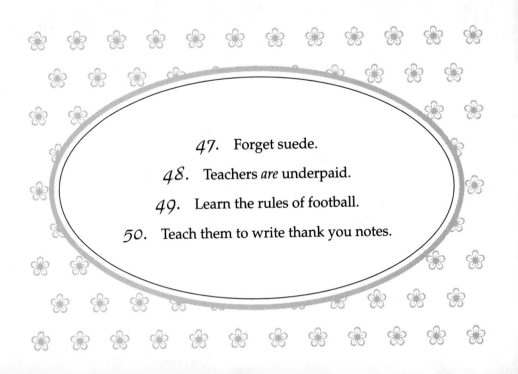

47. Forget suede.

48. Teachers *are* underpaid.

49. Learn the rules of football.

50. Teach them to write thank you notes.

51. Your teenage daughter *will* find you embarrassing.

52. Cheese food is not cheese.

53. Thirteen is too late to put them up for adoption.

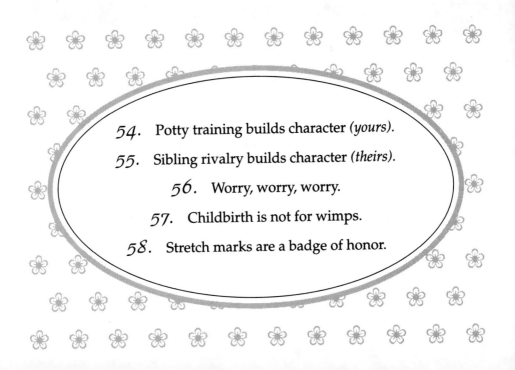

54. Potty training builds character *(yours)*.

55. Sibling rivalry builds character *(theirs)*.

56. Worry, worry, worry.

57. Childbirth is not for wimps.

58. Stretch marks are a badge of honor.

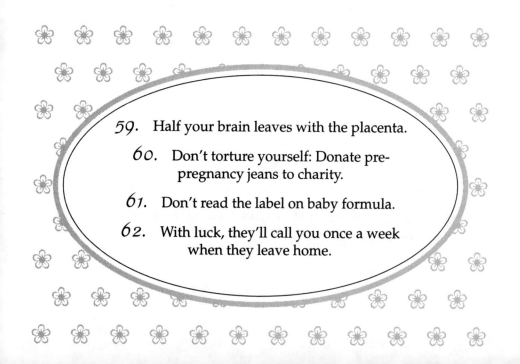

59. Half your brain leaves with the placenta.

60. Don't torture yourself: Donate pre-pregnancy jeans to charity.

61. Don't read the label on baby formula.

62. With luck, they'll call you once a week when they leave home.

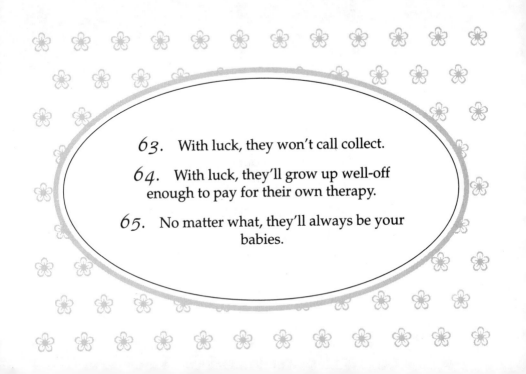

63. With luck, they won't call collect.

64. With luck, they'll grow up well-off enough to pay for their own therapy.

65. No matter what, they'll always be your babies.

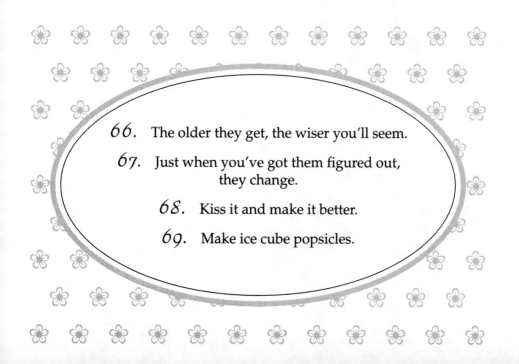

66. The older they get, the wiser you'll seem.

67. Just when you've got them figured out,
    they change.

68. Kiss it and make it better.

69. Make ice cube popsicles.

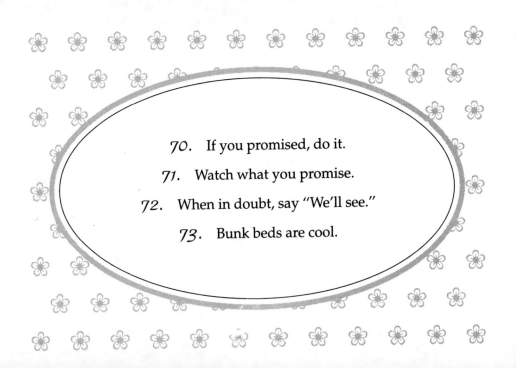

70. If you promised, do it.

71. Watch what you promise.

72. When in doubt, say "We'll see."

73. Bunk beds are cool.

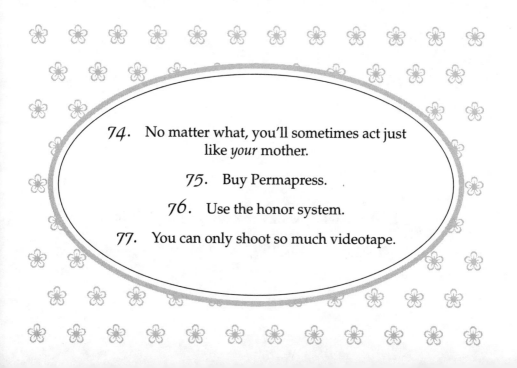

74. No matter what, you'll sometimes act just like *your* mother.

75. Buy Permapress.

76. Use the honor system.

77. You can only shoot so much videotape.

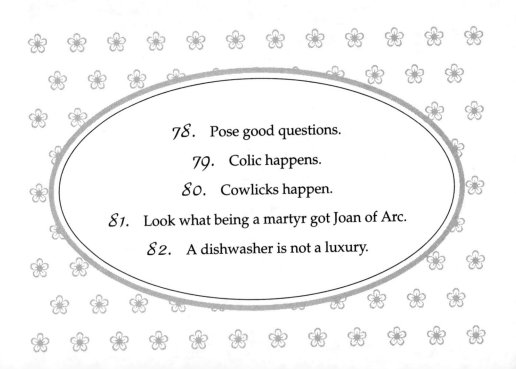

78. Pose good questions.

79. Colic happens.

80. Cowlicks happen.

81. Look what being a martyr got Joan of Arc.

82. A dishwasher is not a luxury.

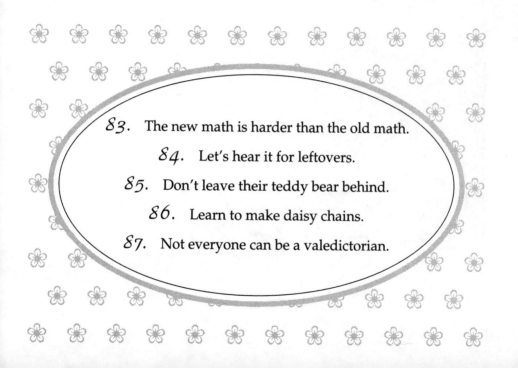

83. The new math is harder than the old math.

84. Let's hear it for leftovers.

85. Don't leave their teddy bear behind.

86. Learn to make daisy chains.

87. Not everyone can be a valedictorian.

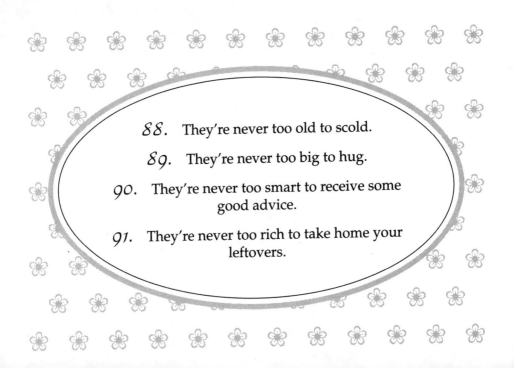

88. They're never too old to scold.

89. They're never too big to hug.

90. They're never too smart to receive some good advice.

91. They're never too rich to take home your leftovers.

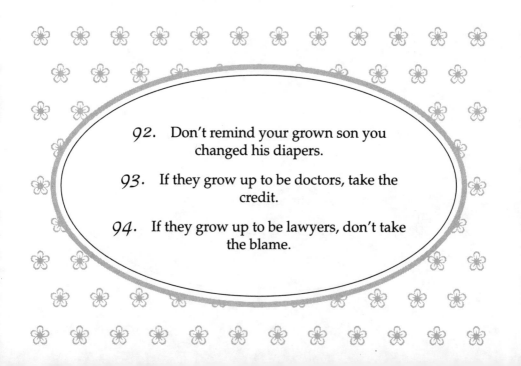

92. Don't remind your grown son you changed his diapers.

93. If they grow up to be doctors, take the credit.

94. If they grow up to be lawyers, don't take the blame.

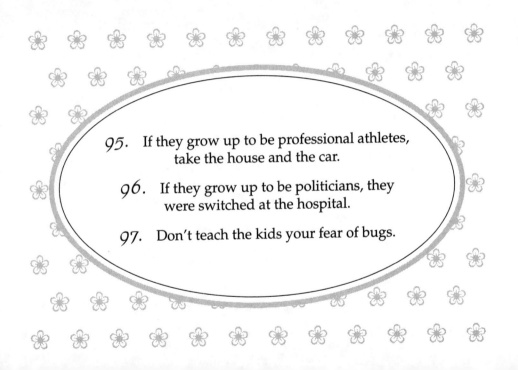

95. If they grow up to be professional athletes, take the house and the car.

96. If they grow up to be politicians, they were switched at the hospital.

97. Don't teach the kids your fear of bugs.

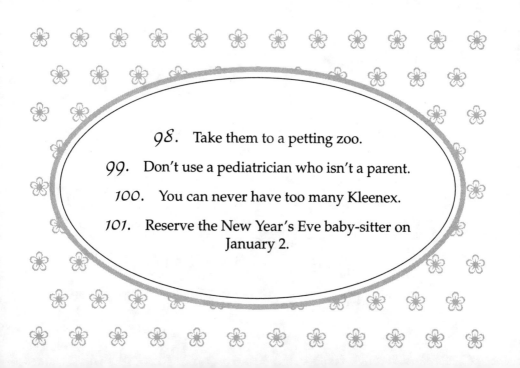

98. Take them to a petting zoo.

99. Don't use a pediatrician who isn't a parent.

100. You can never have too many Kleenex.

101. Reserve the New Year's Eve baby-sitter on January 2.

102. You can blame just about anything on teething.

103. Some of the great minds of our time were bed wetters.

104. Let someone else break the news about Santa Claus.

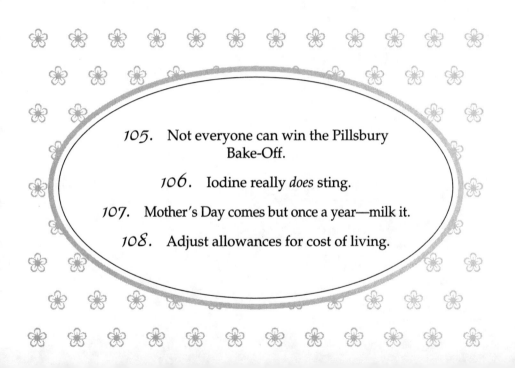

105. Not everyone can win the Pillsbury Bake-Off.

106. Iodine really *does* sting.

107. Mother's Day comes but once a year—milk it.

108. Adjust allowances for cost of living.

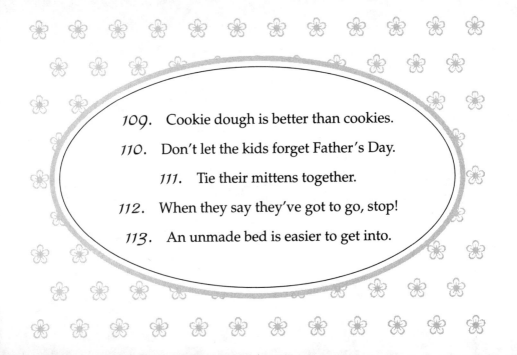

109. Cookie dough is better than cookies.

110. Don't let the kids forget Father's Day.

111. Tie their mittens together.

112. When they say they've got to go, stop!

113. An unmade bed is easier to get into.

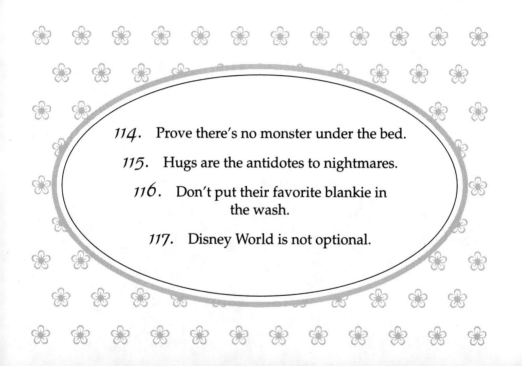

114. Prove there's no monster under the bed.

115. Hugs are the antidotes to nightmares.

116. Don't put their favorite blankie in the wash.

117. Disney World is not optional.

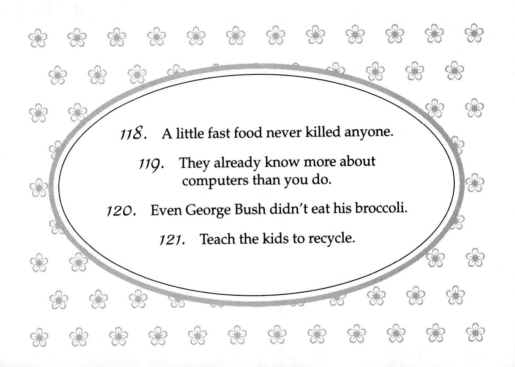

118. A little fast food never killed anyone.

119. They already know more about computers than you do.

120. Even George Bush didn't eat his broccoli.

121. Teach the kids to recycle.

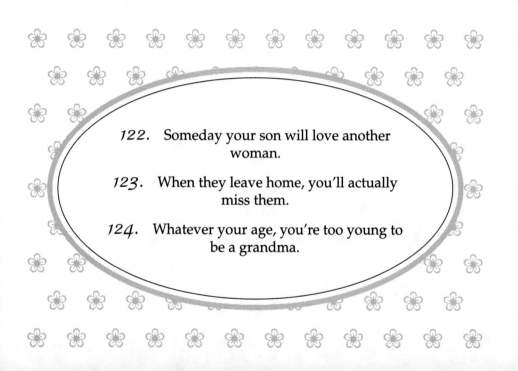

122. Someday your son will love another woman.

123. When they leave home, you'll actually miss them.

124. Whatever your age, you're too young to be a grandma.

125. The more they tease you, the more you're loved.

126. Always make their favorite dish when they visit.

127. Believe it or not, SATs aren't everything.

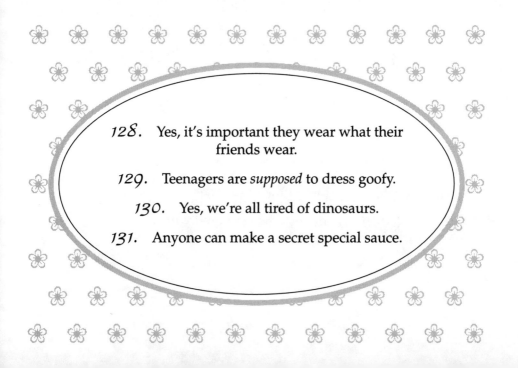

128. Yes, it's important they wear what their friends wear.

129. Teenagers are *supposed* to dress goofy.

130. Yes, we're all tired of dinosaurs.

131. Anyone can make a secret special sauce.

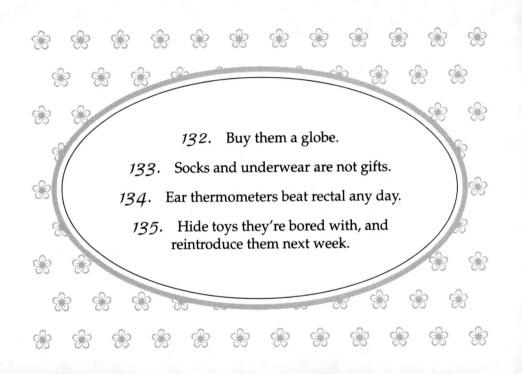

132. Buy them a globe.

133. Socks and underwear are not gifts.

134. Ear thermometers beat rectal any day.

135. Hide toys they're bored with, and reintroduce them next week.

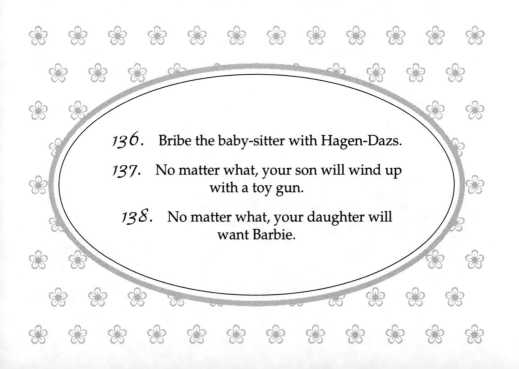

136. Bribe the baby-sitter with Hagen-Dazs.

137. No matter what, your son will wind up with a toy gun.

138. No matter what, your daughter will want Barbie.

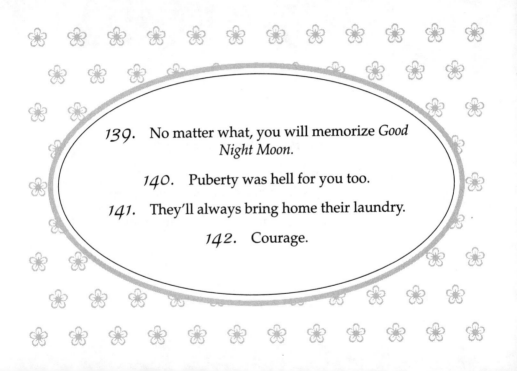

139. No matter what, you will memorize *Good Night Moon.*

140. Puberty was hell for you too.

141. They'll always bring home their laundry.

142. Courage.

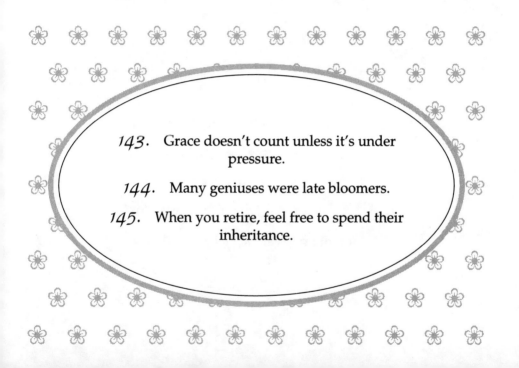

143. Grace doesn't count unless it's under pressure.

144. Many geniuses were late bloomers.

145. When you retire, feel free to spend their inheritance.

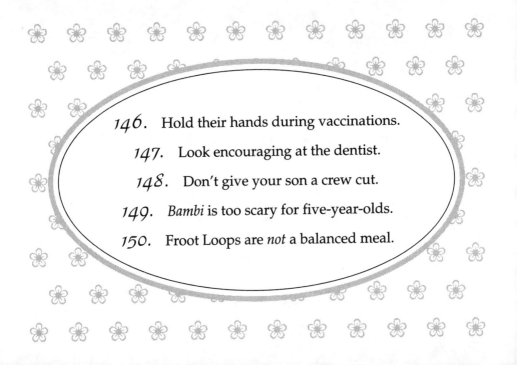

146. Hold their hands during vaccinations.

147. Look encouraging at the dentist.

148. Don't give your son a crew cut.

149. *Bambi* is too scary for five-year-olds.

150. Froot Loops are *not* a balanced meal.

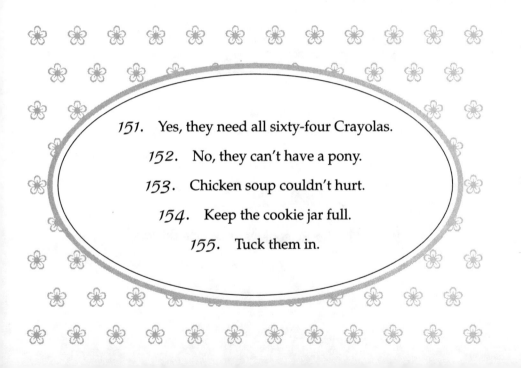

151. Yes, they need all sixty-four Crayolas.

152. No, they can't have a pony.

153. Chicken soup couldn't hurt.

154. Keep the cookie jar full.

155. Tuck them in.

156. Add sound effects to the bedtime story.

157. No, they *really* can't have a pony.

158. Gingerbread houses aren't worth the work.

159. Tollhouse cookies *are* worth the work.

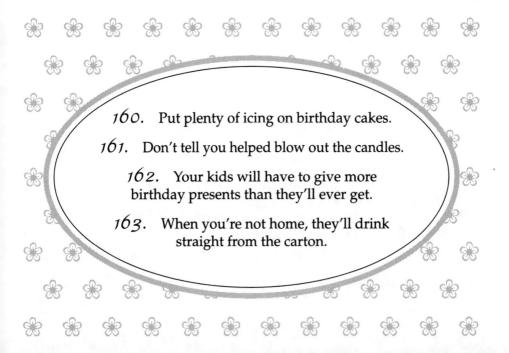

160. Put plenty of icing on birthday cakes.

161. Don't tell you helped blow out the candles.

162. Your kids will have to give more birthday presents than they'll ever get.

163. When you're not home, they'll drink straight from the carton.

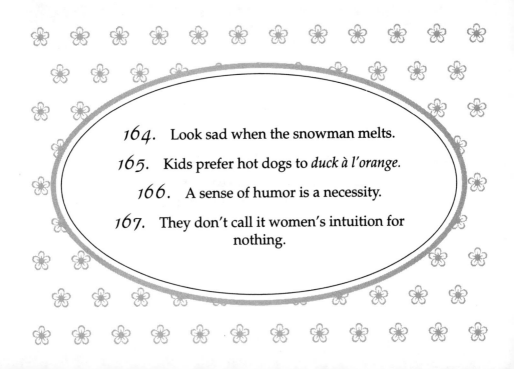

164. Look sad when the snowman melts.

165. Kids prefer hot dogs to *duck à l'orange*.

166. A sense of humor is a necessity.

167. They don't call it women's intuition for nothing.

168. Insist on short-haired dogs.

169. Coax the cat out of the tree.

170. For the last time, a pony is out!

171. Sew name tags in their underwear.

172. Be a den mother.

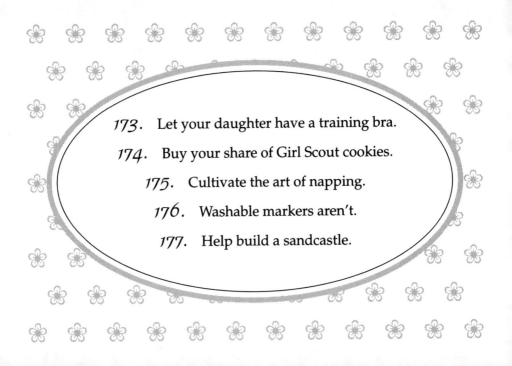

173. Let your daughter have a training bra.

174. Buy your share of Girl Scout cookies.

175. Cultivate the art of napping.

176. Washable markers aren't.

177. Help build a sandcastle.

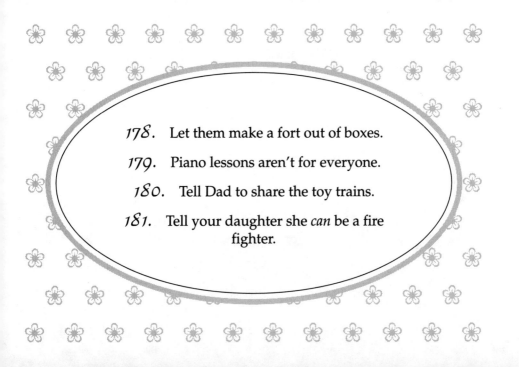

178. Let them make a fort out of boxes.

179. Piano lessons aren't for everyone.

180. Tell Dad to share the toy trains.

181. Tell your daughter she *can* be a fire fighter.

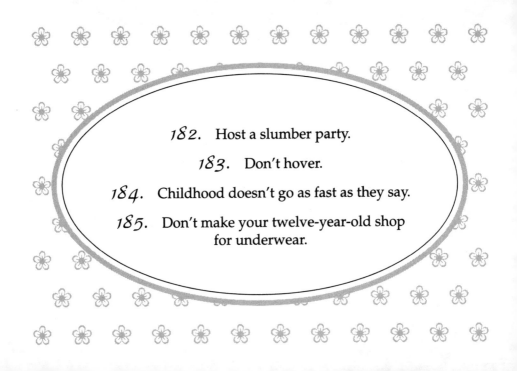

182. Host a slumber party.

183. Don't hover.

184. Childhood doesn't go as fast as they say.

185. Don't make your twelve-year-old shop for underwear.

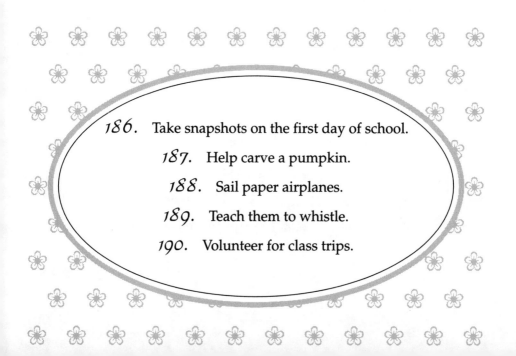

186. Take snapshots on the first day of school.

187. Help carve a pumpkin.

188. Sail paper airplanes.

189. Teach them to whistle.

190. Volunteer for class trips.

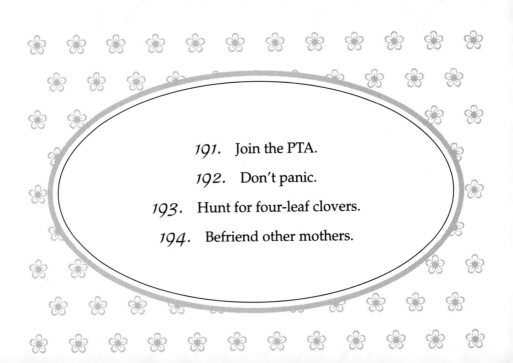

191. Join the PTA.

192. Don't panic.

193. Hunt for four-leaf clovers.

194. Befriend other mothers.

195. Don't let your kids record your answering machine message.

196. Scotchguard everything.

197. There's a little Martha Stewart in all of us.

198. Never use the check-out with the candy display.

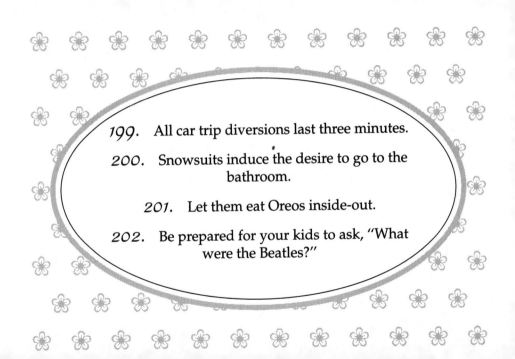

199. All car trip diversions last three minutes.

200. Snowsuits induce the desire to go to the bathroom.

201. Let them eat Oreos inside-out.

202. Be prepared for your kids to ask, "What were the Beatles?"

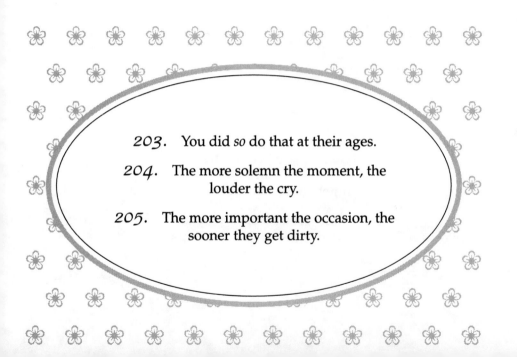

203.   You did *so* do that at their ages.

204.   The more solemn the moment, the louder the cry.

205.   The more important the occasion, the sooner they get dirty.

206. Don't take kids grocery shopping on empty stomachs.

207. Forget your moral objections to pacifiers.

208. Junk food forbidden at home will be consumed at the neighbors.

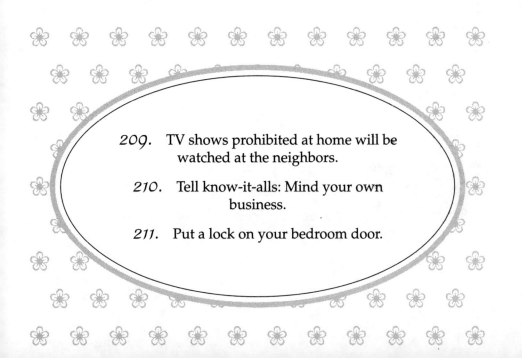

209. TV shows prohibited at home will be watched at the neighbors.

210. Tell know-it-alls: Mind your own business.

211. Put a lock on your bedroom door.

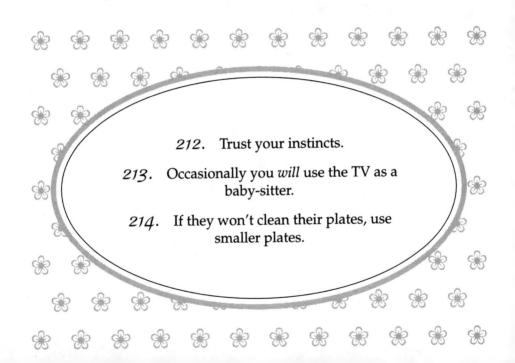

212. Trust your instincts.

213. Occasionally you *will* use the TV as a baby-sitter.

214. If they won't clean their plates, use smaller plates.

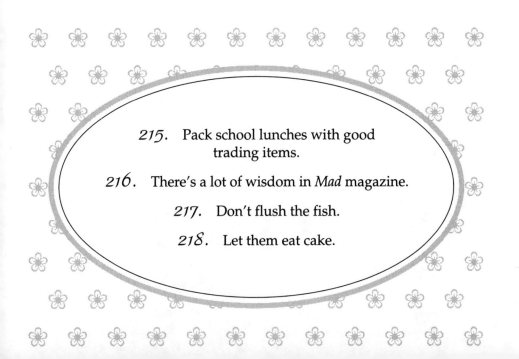

215. Pack school lunches with good trading items.

216. There's a lot of wisdom in *Mad* magazine.

217. Don't flush the fish.

218. Let them eat cake.

219. Let them eat animal crackers.

220. Keep smiling.

221. There's no escaping car pools.

222. Yes, they'll need braces.

223. Yes, they'll need stitches.

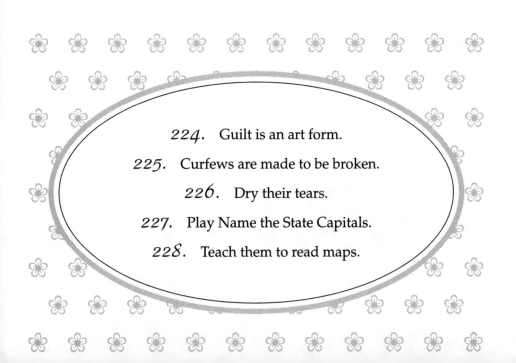

224. Guilt is an art form.

225. Curfews are made to be broken.

226. Dry their tears.

227. Play Name the State Capitals.

228. Teach them to read maps.

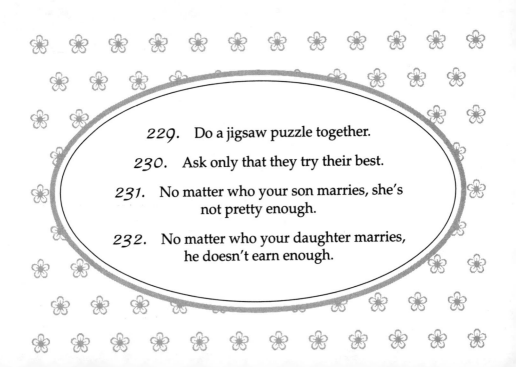

229. Do a jigsaw puzzle together.

230. Ask only that they try their best.

231. No matter who your son marries, she's not pretty enough.

232. No matter who your daughter marries, he doesn't earn enough.

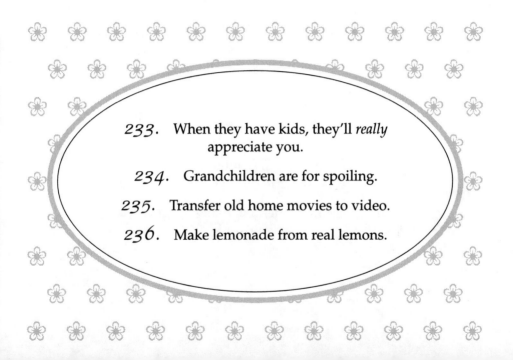

233. When they have kids, they'll *really* appreciate you.

234. Grandchildren are for spoiling.

235. Transfer old home movies to video.

236. Make lemonade from real lemons.

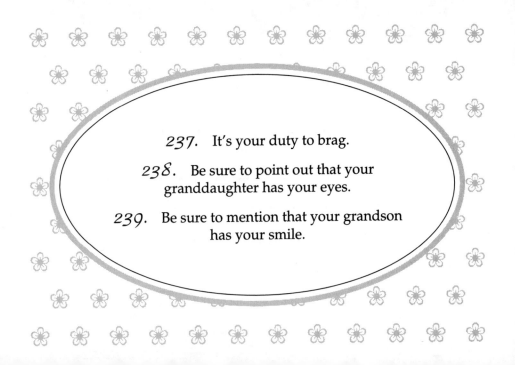

237. It's your duty to brag.

238. Be sure to point out that your granddaughter has your eyes.

239. Be sure to mention that your grandson has your smile.

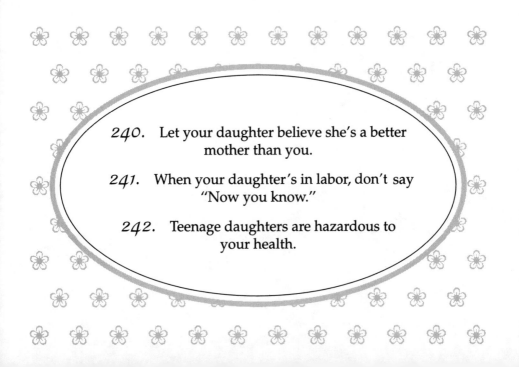

240. Let your daughter believe she's a better mother than you.

241. When your daughter's in labor, don't say "Now you know."

242. Teenage daughters are hazardous to your health.

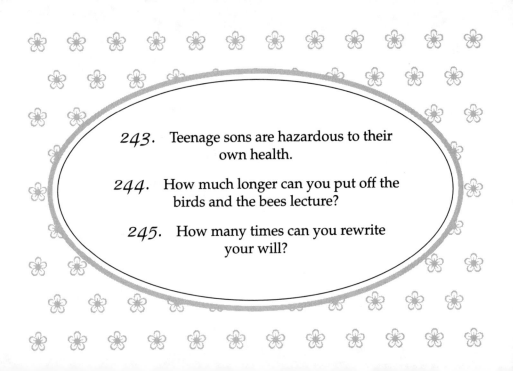

243. Teenage sons are hazardous to their own health.

244. How much longer can you put off the birds and the bees lecture?

245. How many times can you rewrite your will?

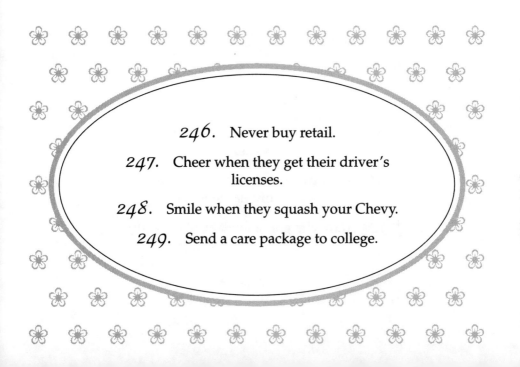

246. Never buy retail.

247. Cheer when they get their driver's licenses.

248. Smile when they squash your Chevy.

249. Send a care package to college.

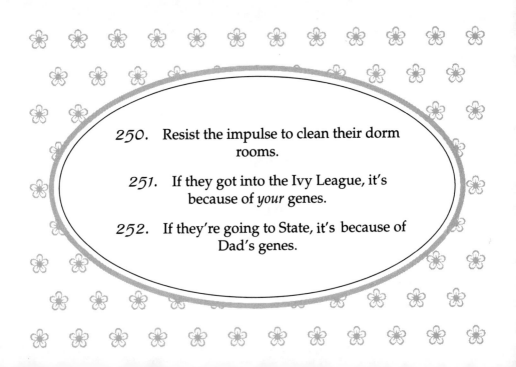

250. Resist the impulse to clean their dorm rooms.

251. If they got into the Ivy League, it's because of *your* genes.

252. If they're going to State, it's because of Dad's genes.

253. Teach them to swim early.

254. Insist on bike helmets.

255. Learn CPR.

256. Take them to the circus.

257. Send an apple for the teacher.

258. No blue hair.

259. Remind them when it's your silver anniversary.

260. Forbid them to put you in a nursing home.

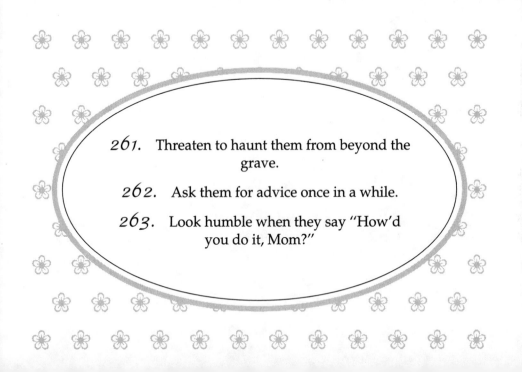

261. Threaten to haunt them from beyond the grave.

262. Ask them for advice once in a while.

263. Look humble when they say "How'd you do it, Mom?"

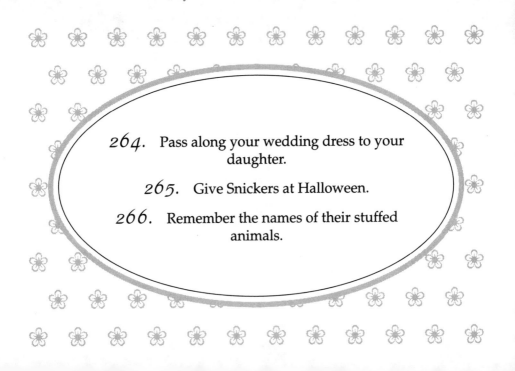

264. Pass along your wedding dress to your daughter.

265. Give Snickers at Halloween.

266. Remember the names of their stuffed animals.

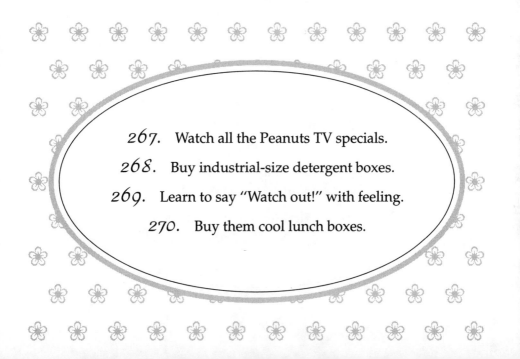

267. Watch all the Peanuts TV specials.

268. Buy industrial-size detergent boxes.

269. Learn to say "Watch out!" with feeling.

270. Buy them cool lunch boxes.

271. Remain calm when you find your son's *Playboy*.

272. Remain calm when you find your daughter's birth control.

273. Your daughter's house will never be as clean as yours.

274. Dance a tango at your child's wedding.

275. Reminisce.

276. Make their Halloween costumes.

277. Play Scrabble with them.

278. Play cards with them.

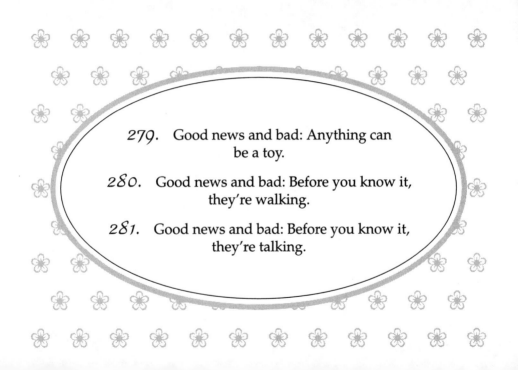

279. Good news and bad: Anything can be a toy.

280. Good news and bad: Before you know it, they're walking.

281. Good news and bad: Before you know it, they're talking.

282. Good news and bad: Before you know it, they're in college.

283. Keep a first-aid kit handy.

284. You and Dad need a "Date Night."

285. Let them make their own sundaes.

286. Don't show their dates naked baby pictures.

287. Traditions are important.

288. Don't forget, each new kid is a tax deduction.

289. Teach them to love libraries.

290. Help start a stamp collection.

291. Give pennies for piggy banks.

292. Learn to love Trolls.

293. Pray for a chicken pox vaccine.

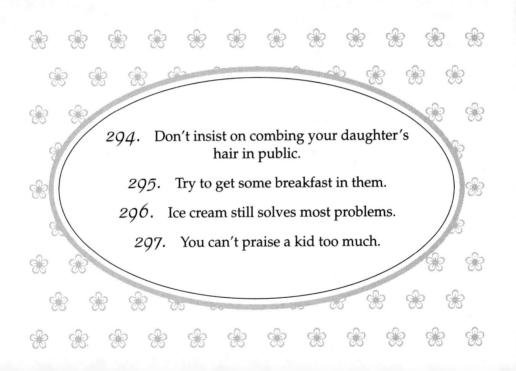

294. Don't insist on combing your daughter's hair in public.

295. Try to get some breakfast in them.

296. Ice cream still solves most problems.

297. You can't praise a kid too much.

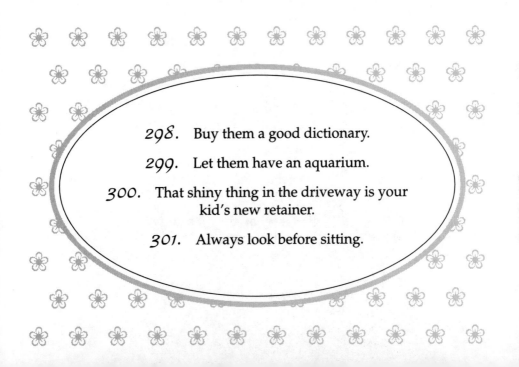

298. Buy them a good dictionary.

299. Let them have an aquarium.

300. That shiny thing in the driveway is your kid's new retainer.

301. Always look before sitting.

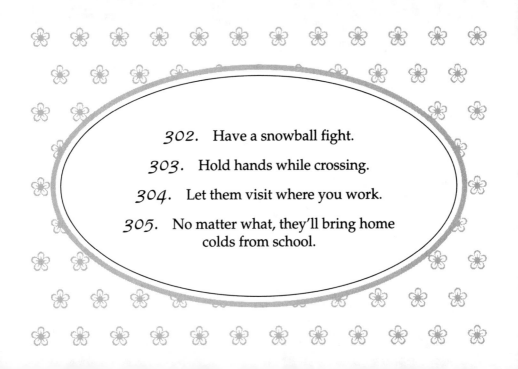

302. Have a snowball fight.

303. Hold hands while crossing.

304. Let them visit where you work.

305. No matter what, they'll bring home colds from school.

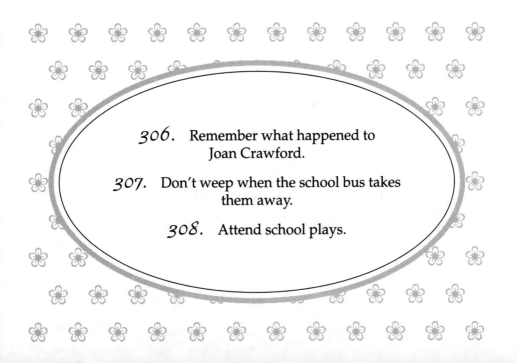

306. Remember what happened to Joan Crawford.

307. Don't weep when the school bus takes them away.

308. Attend school plays.

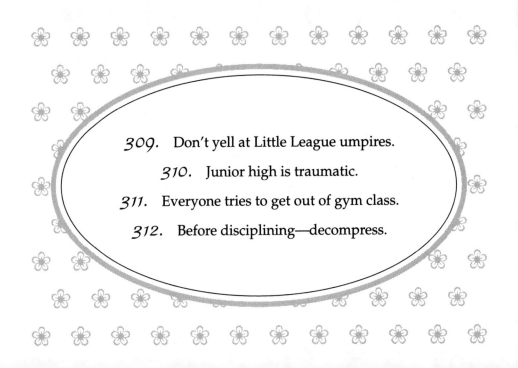

309. Don't yell at Little League umpires.

310. Junior high is traumatic.

311. Everyone tries to get out of gym class.

312. Before disciplining—decompress.

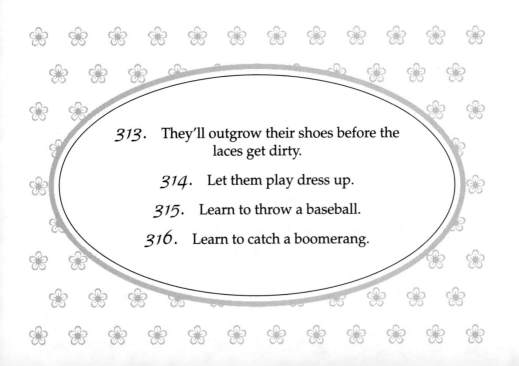

313. They'll outgrow their shoes before the laces get dirty.

314. Let them play dress up.

315. Learn to throw a baseball.

316. Learn to catch a boomerang.

317. If they created it at camp, put it on display.

318. Food fights happen.

319. Get washable wallpaper.

320. Don't let them call you by your first name.

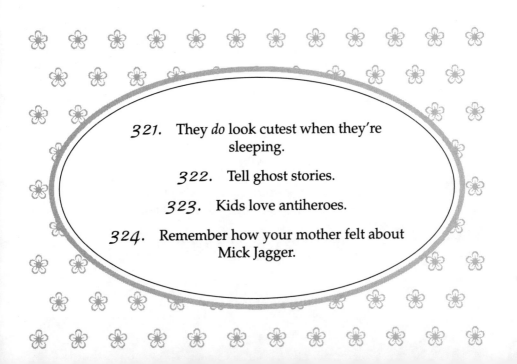

321. They *do* look cutest when they're sleeping.

322. Tell ghost stories.

323. Kids love antiheroes.

324. Remember how your mother felt about Mick Jagger.

325. Celebrate Velcro!

326. Record their singing.

327. You know your daughter's grown up when she stretches out your sweater.

328. You know your son's grown up when he blushes.

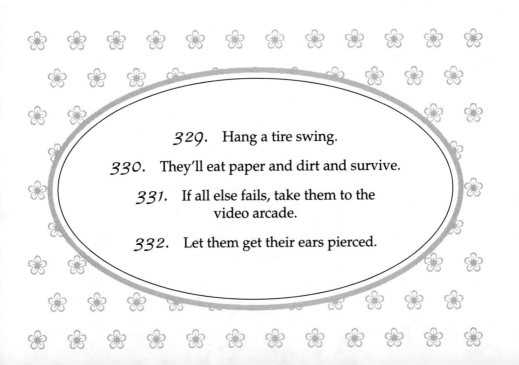

329. Hang a tire swing.

330. They'll eat paper and dirt and survive.

331. If all else fails, take them to the video arcade.

332. Let them get their ears pierced.

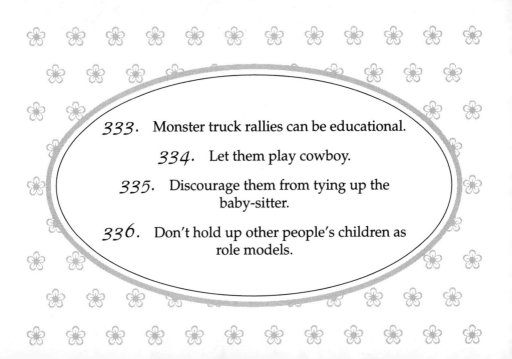

333. Monster truck rallies can be educational.

334. Let them play cowboy.

335. Discourage them from tying up the baby-sitter.

336. Don't hold up other people's children as role models.

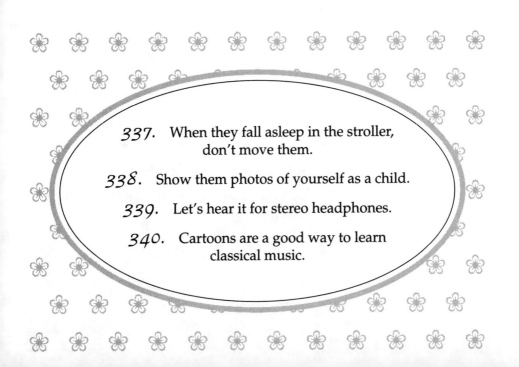

337. When they fall asleep in the stroller, don't move them.

338. Show them photos of yourself as a child.

339. Let's hear it for stereo headphones.

340. Cartoons are a good way to learn classical music.

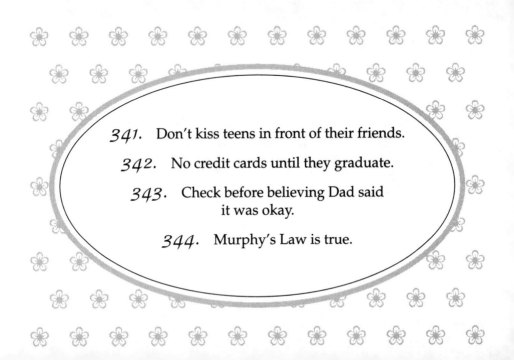

341. Don't kiss teens in front of their friends.

342. No credit cards until they graduate.

343. Check before believing Dad said it was okay.

344. Murphy's Law is true.

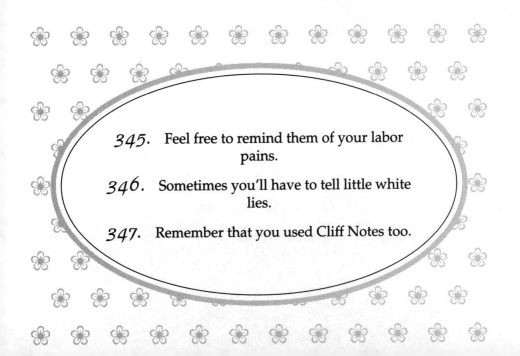

345. Feel free to remind them of your labor pains.

346. Sometimes you'll have to tell little white lies.

347. Remember that you used Cliff Notes too.

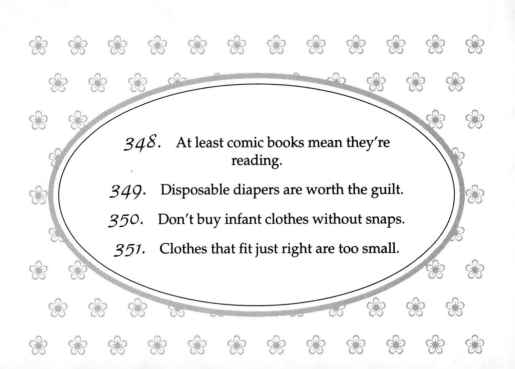

348. At least comic books mean they're reading.

349. Disposable diapers are worth the guilt.

350. Don't buy infant clothes without snaps.

351. Clothes that fit just right are too small.

352. Everybody's a critic.

353. Get call waiting.

354. If you have teenagers, get your own phone.

355. You don't need physicists to tell you about chaos theory.

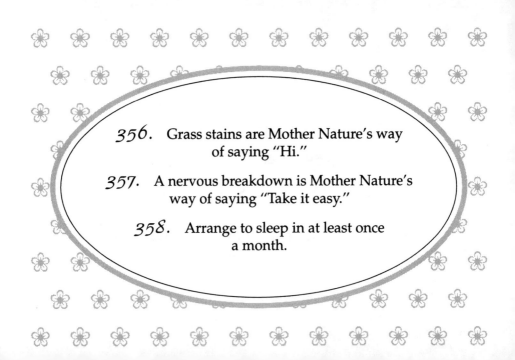

356. Grass stains are Mother Nature's way of saying "Hi."

357. A nervous breakdown is Mother Nature's way of saying "Take it easy."

358. Arrange to sleep in at least once a month.

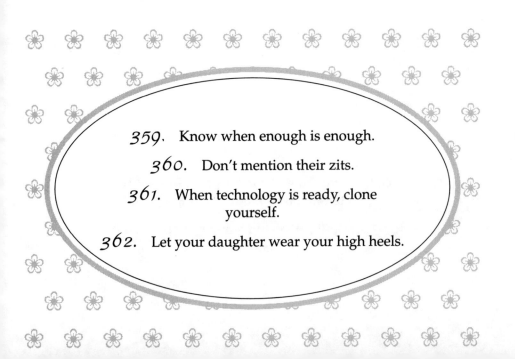

359. Know when enough is enough.

360. Don't mention their zits.

361. When technology is ready, clone yourself.

362. Let your daughter wear your high heels.

363. Admire your son's mustache even if you can't see it.

364. Discourage your offspring from writing a tell-all book about growing up.

365. You'll never stop wondering if you did a good job.